KU-575-603

Fiendishly funny poems

picked by John Foster

Illustrated by Nathan Reed

HarperCollins *Children's Books*

DUDLEY PUBLIC LIBRARIES

L 4790 1

666078 | SCH

J821.08

First published by HarperCollins *Children's Books* in 2004
HarperCollins *Children's Books* is an imprint of HarperCollins*Publishers* Ltd,
77-85 Fulham Palace Road, Hammersmith, W6 8JB

www.harpercollinschildrensbooks.co.uk

1 3 5 7 9 8 6 4 2

This edition copyright © John Foster 2004
Illustrations by Nathan Reed 2004
The acknowledgements on page 95-96
constitute an extension of this copyright page.

ISBN 0 00 714803 8

The authors, illustrator and editor assert the moral right to
be identified as the authors, illustrator and editor of this work.

Printed and bound in England by
Clays Ltd, St Ives plc

Conditions of Sale

Without limiting the rights under copyright reserved above,
this book is sold subject to the condition
that it shall not, by way of trade or otherwise,
be lent, re-sold, hired out or otherwise circulated
without both the publisher's and copyright owner's
prior written consent in any form,
binding or cover other than that in which it is
published and without a similar condition
including this condition being imposed
on the subsequent purchaser.

Contents

THE HAND OF THE SPOOK OF YORK

MONDAY'S CHILD HAS BUILDER'S BUM

OUR LOLLIPOP LADY WEARS A BIKINI

The Bedbugs Are Throwing a Party

The Bedbugs Are Throwing a Party

The bedbugs are throwing a party
And I know who they're going to invite.
So select your best pyjamas
And arrange to stay the night.

You'll be their guest of honour,
The cause of great delight.
If you grace them with your presence
Everything will be just right.

Do accept their invitation
(To refuse would be impolite).
And please be there for the midnight feast –
It's you they're intending to bite!

Bernard Young

Once Bitten

A spider sat on Auntie's chair,
Auntie didn't see it there,
her language was most unrefined
when it bit her large behind.

Michael Dugan

Auntie Babs

Auntie Babs became besotted
With her snake, so nicely spotted,
Unaware that pets so mottled
Like to leave their keepers throttled.

Colin West

The Crocodile

The crocodile has a toothy smile.

He opens his jaws with a grin.

He's very polite

Before taking a bite.

He always says, 'Please come in!'

John Foster

Dining Out With Danger!

When you date an alligator,
tell the chef and tell the waiter
there and then. It's too late later.
Dwell on it, advise them well.

Say your mate's an alligator.
Spell it out: potato-hater;
needs raw meat put on the plate or
eats the staff, and the clientele.

Nick Toczek

Octocure

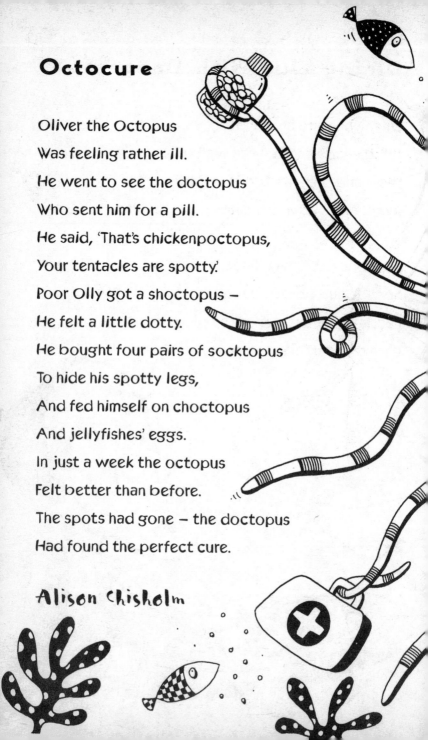

Oliver the Octopus
Was feeling rather ill.
He went to see the doctopus
Who sent him for a pill.
He said, 'That's chickenpoctopus,
Your tentacles are spotty.'
Poor Olly got a shoctopus –
He felt a little dotty.
He bought four pairs of socktopus
To hide his spotty legs,
And fed himself on choctopus
And jellyfishes' eggs.
In just a week the octopus
Felt better than before.
The spots had gone – the doctopus
Had found the perfect cure.

Alison Chisholm

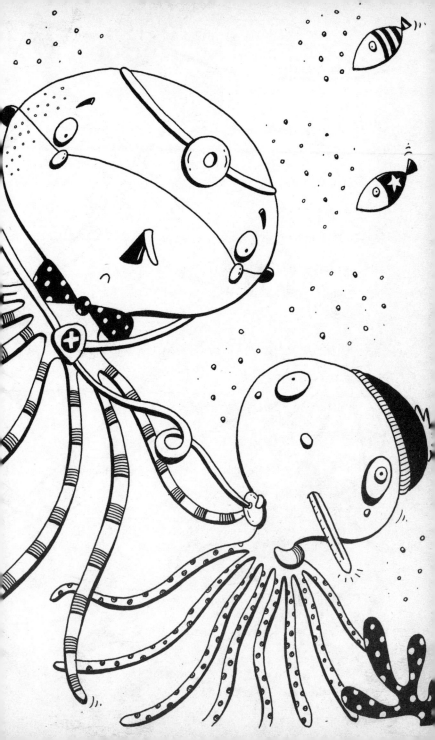

Pterence Pterodactyl and the Ptattoo

Pterence Pterodactyl
Had a pterrible pto-do.
The pto-do was his mother;
It was about a new ptattoo.

'Pterodactyls don't have ptattoos.'
Was his mother's point of view.
'I let you have one last ptime
And ptatty it looks ptoo.'

My friends have more than one,
Thought Pterry feeling blue;
Why can't Pterence Pteredactyl
Ptry ptwo ptatty ptattoos ptoo?

Ptrevor Millum

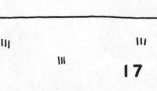

17

A Gnu Who Was New to the Zoo

A gnu who was new to the zoo
Asked another gnu what he should do.
The other gnu said, shaking his head,
'If I knew I'd tell you –
I am a new gnu too!'

John Foster

E-pet-aph

Gerbil Gerry made a mess

When he got trapped in the trouser press.

It's sad to say, the truth is that

Both of us now feel quite flat.

Poor old pet with a permanent crease,

Gerry Gerbil, Pressed in Peace.

Andrew Fusek Peters
and Polly Peters

Getting the Facts Right

A dog that's a boxer is lacking a punch;

A pelican WON'T fit the bill;

And do not believe what some people have said –

A 'sturgeon' WON'T HELP if you're ill!

You can't wash your hands in a bison;

A hyena has NEVER been tall;

And, whatever Darwin or others might say,

The lynx ISN'T 'missing' at all!

Trevor Harvey

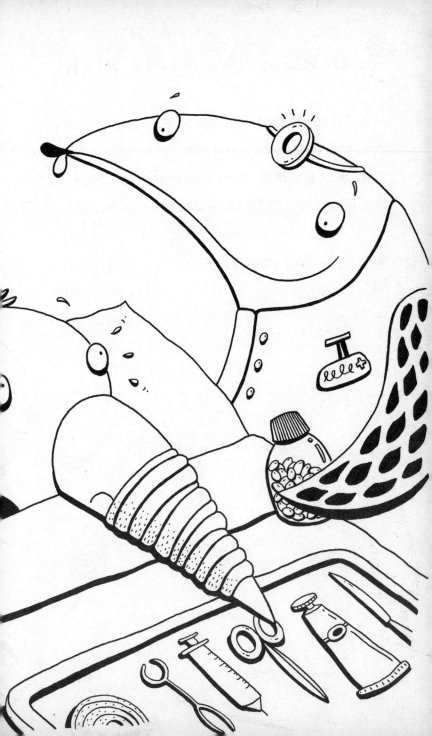

Foul Play

Here lie the bones of one fine hen
Admired by all who saw her
And all these little marks you see
Are where we did all gnaw her.

Patricia Leighton

My Dad Has a Hole in His Hair

My Dad

My dad has a hole in his hair
You can see his pink head quite plain
He says he's had it organised
To let the air cool down his brain

My dad has a hole in his hair
He says it is where he's grown
His hair is where it's always been
So his head's come through in a dome

My dad has a hole in his hair
He's planning for when he gets old
He'll have solar panels fitted
To start up his brain when it's cold

Dad says if I work much harder
And increase the size of my brain
I'll have a hole in my hair like his
And be able to hear the rain

Pat Gadsby

Grilled to Perfection

Little Timmy rushed inside
And yelled out to his mum,
'Dad's fallen on the bonfire,
Quick, you'd better come!'

But Timmy's mum was unperturbed,
She knew just what to do –
'Great, invite your friends around,
We'll have a barbecue...'

Clive Webster

Happy Families

Mr Pill the pharmacist
Mrs Bunn the baker
Master Leak the plumber's mate
B. Grave the undertaker.

Mr Blast, who in the past
once mended broken hooters
Mr Spider – web designer
Miss Take – in computers.

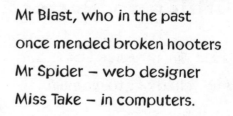

Ena Hurry makes strong curry
Old MacDonald farms
Mr Cue is in the theatre
Bill Ithole sells arms.

Master Void is unemployed
Reg Card – a referee
When I grow up, I worry what
My name suggests I'll be.

What kind of job might go with Robb?
I bet you think you know it.
But I'd rather rhyme that turn to crime
So perhaps I'll be a poet.

Lindsay MacRae

Family Doctor

My grandpa thinks he's a cricket ball.

And, sometimes, he's a bat.

He went and told the Doctor

And the Doctor said, 'Howzat?'

My sister went to the Doctor's,

In front of the Doctor she sat.

She said, 'Doctor, I think I'm invisible!'

And the Doctor said, 'Who said that?'

My uncle went to the Doctor's

'I'm a toadstool!' I heard him shout.

The Doctor said, 'You're a fun guy.

There's not mushroom for doubt!'

My father went to the Doctor's,

He said, 'I'm feeling chronic!'

All I can think of is "Gin, gin, gin!'"

And the Doctor said, 'You need a tonic!'

My brother went to the Doctor's,
He was feeling under the weather.
He said, 'I think I'm some curtains!'
She said, 'Pull yourself together!'

Ian Larmont

Mixed-Up Aunty

When Aunty fell in the concrete mixer
We couldn't find her at all.
Nobody has seen her since,
But her statue's appeared in the hall!

Andrew Collett

My Baby Brother's In Disgrace

My baby brother's in disgrace.
There's water everywhere.
This morning he decided
To wash his teddy's hair.

My baby brother's in disgrace.
He used all the shampoo.
Instead of putting him in the bath,
He showered him in the loo!

John Foster

SP•TTY J•E

He's g•t m•re sp•ts than a le•pard,
m•re sp•ts than a Dalmatian,
he's g•t m•re sp•ts than a cheetah:
he's •ur super-sp•t sensati•n!

He's g•t sp•ts up•n his kneecaps,
he's g•t sp•ts in r•ws and r•ws.
Wh••s g•t sp•ts, yes, l•ts and l•ts?
The answer's Sp•tty J•e.

He's g•t sp•ts up•n his y•u kn•w what,
he's g•t sp•ts y•u kn•w where;
he's great f•r games •f d•t t• d•t –
Sp•tty J•e's g•t sp•ts t• spare.

He's g•t sp•ts up•n his b•tt•m,
he's g•t sp•ts up•n his n•se;
everywhere he's g•t them.
Three cheers f•r Sp•tty J•e!

Mike Johnson

Mistaken Identity

I thought I'd seen a monster
From Outer Outer Space,
'Til Dad said, 'No it's just your mum
With a mudpack on her face...'

Clive Webster

Can You Believe It?

Did you hear

About my grandad Jack?

He bit a sausage

And it bit him back!

Did you hear

About my grandma Joan?

She vanished

Down her mobile phone!

Did you hear

About my uncle Jack?

He ate an elephant

For a morning snack!

Did you hear

About my auntie Rose?

She kept a rabbit

Up her nose!

Did you know
About my brother, Joe?
He flew away
On a jet-black crow!

John Kitching

Never Never Never

Never Never Never...

Wear wellies when you're swimming
Or put jelly in your hair.
Brush your teeth with chilli pepper
Or tease a grizzly bear.

Don't ever think of sitting
On a mountain of red ants
Unless, of course, you want to learn
The itchy scratchy dance.

Don't put stickers on your knickers
They'll come off in the wash
And never ask a hippo
For a friendly game of squash.

Rachel Rooney

Hey Diddle Diddle

Wash your ears! Mum said.

So I took them off,

And stuck them in the washing machine.

Clean your room! Dad said.

So I rolled it up,

And shook it out of the window.

Make the breakfast! my brother said.

So I did –

With bits of balsa wood and modelling glue.

Feed the cat! my auntie said,

So I fed him...

To the dog!

Take your time! Dad said.

So I packed up the clocks

And flew off to Mars

Where the days fly by,

Wearing nothing but stars!

Andrew Fusek Peters

Adrian

Has everyone met Adrian?

He really is a hoot.

I gave a birthday party

So he wore his birthday suit.

Colin West

Why Is a Bottom called a Bottom?

Why Is a Bottom Called a Bottom?

If the bottom of my body

Is the bit that's on the ground...

Why's my bottom called my bottom

When it's only half way down?

The top of my body is my head,

This really is a riddle...

Cos the bottom of my body is my feet

So my bottom should be... my middle!

Paul Cookson

Insides

I'm very grateful to my skin
For keeping all my insides in –
I do so hate to think about
What I would look like inside-out.

Colin West

Georgie Porgie

Georgie Porgie, pudding and peas,
had extremely knobbly knees,
but what made all the girls feel queasy
was that his feet smelled awfully cheesy.

Nigel Gray

You Can't Teach an Old Cow New Tricks

Pat-a-cake, pat-a-cake, farmer's man.
Make me a dung heap as fast as you can.
Prick it and pat it and bang it down hard,
And don't go and drop bits all over the yard.

'Farmer, Sir, Farmer, Sir, please may I ask:
Can't we abolish this smelly old task?
Babies use potties, Puss digs little holes;
Why can't our cattle drop theirs into bowls?'

Don't talk such nonsense, my dear farmer's man.
How can a cow learn to sit on a pan?
Don't waste your time by inventing a loo
For cows who would only protest, 'Moo, moo,
MOO!'

Alan Hayward

The Lookout Bird

The lookout bird is quite unique
It has a trunk instead of a beak.
Wrinkly skin where feathers should be
And ears the size of Tennessee.

The lookout bird does not have wings
It cannot fly and never sings
Instead of two it has four legs
Its babies don't come out of eggs.

The lookout bird is well renowned
For dropping bundles on the ground
And if it ventures down your street
Just lookout where you put your feet.

Granville Lawson

Jack

Jack be nimble,
Jack be quick,
Jack jump over
the baby's sick.

David Horner

Little Jack Horner

Little Jack Horner
Has weeeeeed
In the corner.
If you see his mother,
You maybe should warn her!

John Kitching

The Hand of the
Spook of York

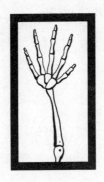

The Hand of the Spook of York

The hand of the Spook of York
Is only seen now and then,
Sometimes it is holding a feather quill,
Sometimes it is holding a pen.

And when one writes the word UP,
And the other writes the word DOWN,
They can't remember which way's up,
So it ends up upside down!

Mike Elliott

Nightmare

I had a nightmare in the night.
I woke up hot and screaming.
The monster sitting on my bed, said,
'Calm down! You're only dreaming.'

Geraldine Aldridge

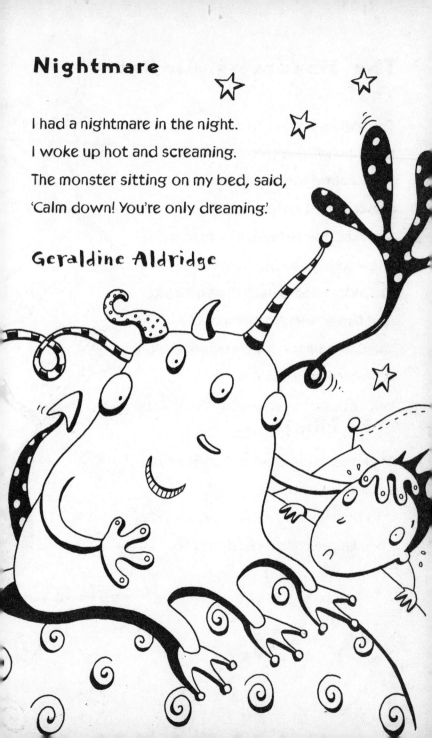

The Screaming Ab-Dab

The Willies and the Collywobbles
took a walk one day
but a horrid Heebie Jeebie came
and frightened them away.
Too late, the Heebie Jeebie heard
a fearsome, fiendish shout.
'Oh, no,' the Heebie Jeebie bawled,
'the Screaming Ab-Dab's out!'
The Screaming Ab-Dab bowled along,
its face a fiery red
but tripped upon a goosebump bush
and landed on its head.
Then the Willies and the Collywobbles
trundled out to scoff
and the Heebie Jeebie split its sides
then laughed its head right off.

Marian Swinger

I am Scallywag the Skeleton

I am Scallywag the Skeleton

And it's heebie-jeebie time,

For the midnight moonlight's shining through the trees.

But it's horrid being hollow

The wind whistles through my ribs

And I'm leaking 'coz I've had a cup of tea!

I used to laugh my head off,

Put my skull on up-side-down,

I would hula-hoop my hips to keep me fit.

Now I'm a mouldy oldie,

Odds and ends are dropping off,

I've already lost a few important bits!

My skull has started sulking,

My knees are front to back,

I need breaking down then building up again.

I'm a crazy kind of jigsaw,

I'm bony building blocks –

Wow, I might just be the latest trendy game!

Maureen Haselhurst

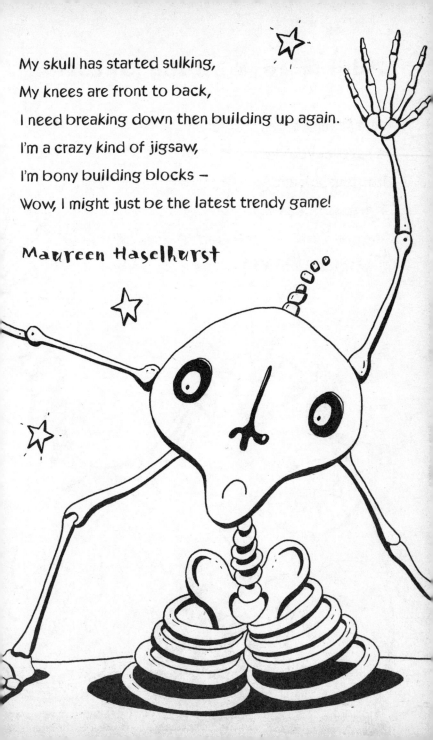

Advice to a Young Ghost

'Please remember,
Whatever you do,
Don't spook until
You're spooken to.'

Trevor Harvey

The Magician's Ghost

The ghost of the magician said,
'I'm really in a fix.
The trouble is the audience
Sees right through all my tricks.'

John Foster

The Inspection

The day the in-spectres turned up here
We knew it was going to be tough.
The problem was that our behaviour
Was simply not dreadful enough.

The headless headmaster took action.
He hatched out a plan for the school
And passed it around in a leaflet
Entitled 'Guidelines for the ghoul'.

Your wailing is weak and infrequent
Your walking through walls could improve.
I'd like to hear more creaking handles
I'd like to see more objects move.
You must make more effort to vanish.
At least, slowly fade out from sight.
I don't want to see you in lessons
Unless your appearance is right.
The way that you play in the playground

58

Is really not shocking me much.
Try harder to creep up on classmates
And grab with a cold clammy touch.
In PE, you must wear the full kit
So here's a reminder once more
Just slip on a white sheet with eye holes
And chains that reach down to the floor.

We followed these guidelines with gusto
Each time the in-spectres were there.
The head (and his body) were dead pleased
He literally floated on air.

Their visit was over quite quickly
They left on the Monday at two.
We thought they'd be here until Friday.
I think we impressed them. Don't you?

Rachel Rooney

My Mummy

My mummy is a Mummy,
She's very tightly wrapped,
And if I touch her bandages,
I get my fingers slapped.

Kaye Umansky

A Dyslexic Wizard

A dyslexic wizard called Og
Found reading his spell book a slog
He shouted out, 'Croak!'
When he should have said, 'Cloak'
And promptly turned into a frog.

Richard Caley

The Footskull Match

The match was fixed for half-past three
On the eve of Hallowe'en;
A stranger pair of footskull teams
Had never yet been seen.

Spooks and spectres stood in line,
Facing the opposition
Of monsters, ghosts and skeletons:
Haunters v Apparitions.

But this wasn't FOOTBALL — don't be confused,
A different game, you see.
No sign of a ball or leather boots,
Not even a referee.

The 'ball' was really a plastic skull,
Sold in packs of three
At Phantom & Mason, the posh sports shop,
As 'Buy 2, Get 1 Free'.

Straight from the kickoff a goal was scored,

By Bonesy the skeleton,

Who took off HIS skull and kicked it through,

So the score stood at zero-one.

'FOUL!' roared the crowd. 'Send him off!'

But, oh dear, there was no referee.

So the goal was allowed and the score remained;

The Haunters had to agree.

Then Graham the ghoul-keeper strayed from his post,

A foolish thing to do;

And the skull was whammed in by Gavin the ghost,

The score stood at zero-two.

Next Sidney the spook made a wonderful score

By slipping the skull-ball through,

And the spectre-tors gathered let out a great roar

As the score reached one goal to two.

The tension was high now as full time drew near;
The Haunters were desperate for more.
Apparitions would thrash them if they didn't come
   through –
To win they just HAD to score!

There were just seconds left to the end of the match
When Phan-Tom slammed the skull-ball
Right through the ghoul-post; it was a dead cert!
And the final score rose to two-all.

The after-match 'do' was a rowdy affair
Till the sun began to appear.
The ghouls just dissolved with a plaintive wail:
'We must have a re-play next y...'

Collette Drifte

The Handsome Prince

I was walking down a country lane
when a frog jumped out of a ditch.
He said, 'I've had a spell put on me
by a wicked witch.'

He said, 'I am a handsome prince
and if you will be my bride,
you'll break the spell and you can live
forever by my side.'

'We'll live in a magic castle
built of pure white stone.
You'll wear dresses made of finest silk
and sit on a golden throne.'

I said, 'I am not tempted
by the things of which you speak.
I'd rather have a talking frog
any day of the week!'

Geraldine Aldridge

Riddle

Can you make a witch itch?

Take away her W
Then she'll cease to trouble you.

Marian Swinger

Monday's Child Has Builder's Bum

Builder's Bum

Monday's child has builder's bum.

Tuesday's child has a rumbly tum.

Wednesday's child has a runny nose.

Thursday's child has smelly toes.

Friday's child is crabby and scabby.

Saturday's child is fat and flabby.

But the child who thinks he's cool and haughty

Has a face all green and warty.

Brenda Williams

tuesday

wednesday

thursday

friday

saturday

Sunday?

Doctor Foster

A confused Doctor Foster
(who'd been looking for Gloucester)
said, 'This puddle is really gigantic!'
for he'd got the wrong turn
off the M61
and had ended up in the Atlantic!

Colin Macfarlane

Little Bo Peep

Little Bo Peep
Has lost her beep
And doesn't know where to find it;
Her mobile phone
Is out on loan
With a friend she asked to mind it.

Tim Hopkins

The Queen of Hearts

The Queen of Hearts
She stole some darts
Her empty life's now full:
Just watch her check out one-two-nine –
Twenty-five... treble... bull...

Tim Hopkins

Sing a Song of Sixpence

Sing a song of sixpence, a pocket full of rye,

four and twenty blackbirds are baked in a pie.

Before the pie was opened, the birds began to shout:

'It's getting rather hot in here... can someone let us out?'

Colin Macfarlane

Martin Melly and Kitty Kelly

Martin Melly and Kitty Kelly
ate a DVD and a widescreen telly.
Now Martin Melly and Kitty Kelly
watch cartoons on each other's belly.

John Rice

A Glance At the Menu

Potatoes in their jackets
With the special of the day?
Potatoes in their jackets?
Whatever next? I say.

Sprouts in their pyjamas?
Tomatoes dressed in shirts?
Peas in tartan anoraks?
Broccoli in skirts?
Cauliflower with socks on?
Baseball-capped green beans?
Onions wearing overcoats?
Carrots wearing jeans?

Potatoes in their jackets? No,
I don't want dressed-up food.
Waiter, bring me something else,
And this time something nude.

Richard Edwards

Fast Food

At the burger shop
they sell fast food –

Hot dogs sprint
the hundred metres
in ten seconds flat.
Fat chicken nuggets
set the pace
for Olympic races.
Hamburgers hurtle
over hurdles.
Burly baked potatoes
star in the decathlon,
flexing their muscles.
And no one dares tussle
with grilled sausages
that fare well
in a marathon.

Yes, the food is so fast
it's past your lips
before you can ask
for a bag of chips.

Pie Corbett

Fruity Facts

Oh, there aren't any bones in an orange,

An orange is a boneless fruit,

That's why you'll never see an orange

Dressed up in an evening suit,

That's why you'll never find an orange

With knees or nose or chin,

Oh, there aren't any bones in an orange

BUT

It does have a nubbly skin.

Clare Bevan

Our Lollipop Lady Wears a Bikini

Our Lollipop Lady Wears a Bikini

Our lollipop lady wears a bikini,
it's really quite a sight,
for she said her big white coat
was always much too tight.

It's really big and comfy
and now she's never hot
but what it does best of all
is to make all the drivers stop!

Andrew Collett

My Pen Ran Out

Today at school my pen ran out,
so before it was too late,
I ran outside to stop it
from getting past the gate.

Andrew Collett

Mary Had a Little Lamb

Mary had a little lamb, its fleece was white as
   snow,
it followed her to school one day (a fact I'm sure
   you know).
But just before the teacher showed the creature
   out the door
it kindly left its 'calling card' upon the classroom
   floor!

And, after class, the little lass was forced to beg
   its pardon
for having eaten all the flowers in teacher's little
   garden.
At swimming class that afternoon she felt a proper
   fool...
it took the teacher half an hour to fish it out the
   pool!

And later, in the changing room, she heard the
    teacher curse
on finding out the little beast had eaten up her
    purse.
Mary had a little lamb, she hasn't seen it since...
for next day, in the dining hall, they served the
    pupils mince!

Colin Macfarlane

Mistaken Identity

The police came to our school today
They came in at playtime
While Miss was drinking her tea in the staffroom
They marched her off – as we watched
Noses squashed against the playground fence
Then the whispers began.

After play, Mr Stephens our head teacher took us
  for science
The whispers spread silently.

Then just before lunchtime, Mrs Roberts came in and spoke to Mr Stephens

Then he turns to us.

'Children, I'd just like to let you know that the police have informed us that it has all been a case of "Miss taken identity".'

I couldn't believe it.

Miss?

How could she?

Why would she steal somebody else's identity?

Daniel Phelps

Revolting

'It's a full-scale pupil revolt, headmaster.
They're screaming and shouting, "Kids rule!"
Desperate measures are needed, headmaster:
They've got science teachers tied up in the lab
And they're shaving off beards and moustaches;
4C have their teacher roped to the fence
And he's sentenced to twenty-five lashes.
3B's Mr Benbow is walking the plank
Over our vile, slimy pool
While all PE teachers do five hundred press-ups –
Sir, it's chaos out there in the school.
Lady teachers are all forced to eat the school dinners –
And we all know that that's not a laugh –
In this uprising, sir, the kids will be winners:
There's no chance for you and the staff.
Action is needed. I'd strongly advise you
To lock yourself up in the loo.
The staff room's fixed up as a torture chamber
And they're talking of coming for you.'

Eric Finney

A Long, Hard Lesson

Well yes Mr Jones – Toby was here
He went to do a job for me – oh dear
I forgot he was leaving at two – for his holiday
Even though he's told me every single day
This year!

Don't know where he's got to – can't guess
You've missed the plane – what a mess...
I asked him in science – because he was late
To go and ask Miss King for a 'big long weight'
I'd ask Miss King... if I were you.

Daniel Phelps

There Once Was a Teacher From Crewe

There once was a teacher from Crewe
Who gave her class too much to do;
They had 'spellings' galore –
SIXTEEN HUNDRED AND FOUR! –
And when they were done, they said, 'PHEW!'

Trevor Harvey

Spelling Test

The worst thing
to get
in a spelling test
is diarrhoea.

Andy Seed

Enquire Within

'Is there anybody there?' asked the pupil,
Knocking on the staffroom door.
'You'll be lucky!' the cleaner answered.
'It's almost ten past four!'

Trevor Harvey

Acknowledgements

We are grateful to the following authors for permission to include the following poems, all of which are published for the first time in this collection:

Geraldine Aldridge: 'Nightmare' and 'The Handsome Prince' copyright © Geraldine Aldridge 2004. Clare Bevan: 'Fruity Facts' copyright © Clare Bevan 2004. Richard Caley: 'A Dyslexic Wizard' copyright © Richard Caley 2004. Alison Chisholm: 'Octocure' copyright © Alison Chisholm 2004. Andrew Collett: 'Mixed-Up Aunty', 'Our Lollipop Lady Wears a Bikini' and 'My Pen Ran Out' all copyright © Andrew Collett 2004. Collette Drifte: 'The Footskull Match' copyright © Collette Drifte 2004. Michael Dugan: 'Once Bitten' copyright © Michael Dugan 2004. Mike Elliott: 'The Hand of the Spook of York' copyright © Mike Elliott 2004. Eric Finney: 'Revolting' copyright © Eric Finney 2004. John Foster: 'The Magician's Ghost', 'The Crocodile', 'My Baby Brother's in Disgrace' and 'A Gnu Who Was New to the Zoo' all copyright © John Foster 2004. Pat Gadsby: 'My Dad' copyright © Pat Gadsby 2004. Nigel Gray: 'Georgie Porgie' copyright © Nigel Gray 2004. Trevor Harvey: 'Getting the Facts Right' and 'There Once Was a Teacher From Crewe' both copyright © Trevor Harvey 2004. Maureen Haselhurst: 'I am Scallywag the Skeleton' copyright © Maureen Haselhurst 2004. Tim Hopkins: 'The Queen of Hearts' and 'Little Bo Peep' both copyright © Tim Hopkins 2004. David Horner: 'Jack' copyright © David Horner 2004. Mike Johnson: 'SP•TTY J•E' copyright © Mike Johnson 2004. John Kitching: 'Little Jack Horner' and 'Can You Believe It?' both copyright © John Kitching 2004. Ian Larmont: 'Family Doctor' copyright © Ian Larmont 2004. Granville Lawson: 'The Lookout Bird' copyright © Granville Lawson 2004. Patricia Leighton: 'Foul Play' copyright © Patricia Leighton 2004. Colin Macfarlane: 'Doctor Foster', 'Sing a Song of Sixpence' and 'Mary Had a Little Lamb' all copyright © Colin Macfarlane 2004. Trevor Millum: 'Pterence Pterodactyl and the Ptatoo' copyright © Trevor Millum 2004. Daniel Phelps: 'Mistaken Identity' and 'A Long, Hard Lesson' both copyright © Daniel Phelps 2004. John Rice: 'Martin Melly and Kitty Kelly' copyright © John Rice 2004. Rachel Rooney: 'Never Never Never' and 'The Inspection' both copyright © Rachel Rooney 2004. Andy Seed: 'Spelling Test' copyright © Andy Seed 2004. Marian Swinger: 'Riddle' and 'The Screaming Ab-Dab' both copyright © Marian

Swinger 2004. Tick Toczek: 'Dining Out With Danger!' copyright ©
Nick Toczek 2004. Clive Webster: 'Grilled to Perfection' copyright ©
Clive Webster 2004. Colin West: 'Adrian', 'Auntie Babs' and 'Insides'
all copyright © Colin West 2004. Brenda Williams: 'Builder's Bum'
copyright © Brenda Williams 2004.

We also acknowledge permission to include previously published poems:

Paul Cookson: 'Why Is a Bottom Called a Bottom?' copyright © Paul
Cookson 1995, from *Body Poems* compiled by John Foster (Oxford
University Press). Pie Corbett: 'Fast Food' copyright © Pie Corbett
2001, from *Sling a Jammy Doughnut* compiled by Joan Poulson
(Wayland) included by permission of the author. Trevor Harvey:
'Advice to a Young Ghost' copyright © Trevor Harvey 2000, first pub-
lished in *Spectacular Spooks* compiled by Brian Moses (Macmillan)
and 'Enquire Within' copyright © Trevor Harvey, first published in
Funny Poems edited by Heather Amery (Usborne), both included
by permission of the author. Alan Hayward: 'You Can't Teach an Old
Cow New Tricks' copyright © Alan Hayward 1997, from *Fun Poems*
(Summersdale Publishers) included by permission of the author.
Lindsay MacRae: 'Happy Families' copyright © 2000 Lindsay
MacRae from *How To Avoid Kissing Your Parents in Public* (Puffin)
included by permission of the author. Andrew Fusek Peters and
Polly Peters: 'E-pet-aph' copyright © 2001 Andrew Fusek Peters
and Polly Peters, first published in *Sadderday and Funday* (Hodder
Wayland) included by permission of the authors. Andrew Fusek
Peters: 'Hey Diddle Diddle' copyright © 1995 Andrew Fusek Peters,
first broadcast on *Poetry Please* included by permission of the
author. Kaye Umansky: 'My Mummy' copyright © Kaye Umansky
1988, first published in *Witches in Stitches* (Puffin), included by permission of the author. Clive Webster: 'Mistaken Identity' copyright ©
Clive Webster from *Monster Poems* (Oxford University Press)
included by permission of the author. Bernard Young: 'The Bedbugs
Are Throwing a Party' copyright © Bernard Young 1999 from
Minibeasts chosen by Brian Moses (Macmillan) included by permission of the author.